Far Pitched Tents
Poems of War
Second Edition

Michael M. Nikoletseas

2   FAR PITCHED TENTS-POEMS OF WAR

ISBN: 9798857308417

Published in USA

3 FAR PITCHED TENTS-POEMS OF WAR

4 FAR PITCHED TENTS-POEMS OF WAR

Thunder wrote his name on your lips, I know
An eagle built his nest in your eyes, I know
But on this moist river bank there is only one
road
Only one ambiguous road and you mass travel
it
You must wade in blood before time overtakes
you
You must pass to other side to join your
comrades again
Blossoms birds deer
You must find another ocean another serenity
You nust grab the straps of Achilles' horses

Amorgos by Nikos Gatsos, 1943
Translation by Michael Nikoletsea

6 FAR PITCHED TENTS-POEMS OF WAR

The journey

When the sun leaned it broke
it was fall

the men made a ladder
for the howling dog to reach the moon

deep below
the watermill froze

even deeper
the water
turbulent
punctate nebulas
sprayed my viscera

My grandfather
supine
set out on his journey
home

The petit miller

I missed the trough
I poured my grains into the river

running away from the miller's wrath
along the ditch that feeds
the mouths of the world
I charmed the water snakes

set never to return home
I was captured
by Achilles´ mother

9 FAR PITCHED TENTS-POEMS OF WAR

My beret

And I put on my beret
without a badge
and I ran away to war

which army
mother?

Last stroll

When I looked east
the world ended on the face of the cave
still bearing the wrinkles of my grandma

a cow
drained the shadows of the cypress trees
and danced in the red rust of the road
swaying

your last stroll it said
the one before

My orchard

I lay in the sun
palpating the water
running in the orange trees
above

when in the ditch
I saw Tom Sawyer
chasing mystic eels

Hand wisdom

I cut the stone square
I walked behind
I saw the sun

I cut the stone round
I returned
I saw myself

Far pitched tents

I met you again
as on the first time

stench of blood
and war cries
in far pitched tents

Babbling owl

Between me and you
worlds carves my void

when I dissected your face
an owl was born
a babbling apparition

when the torrent ebbs
erect a phallus in a cave
hang my head on the wall
it said

sanctus to naked warriors

Seven beads

I ambushed you at dawn
when dreams are sweet

I adorned your neck
with seven beads of pearl
one for every year of my worship

all night I prayed to you
and weaved songs of valor

at dawn I rooted your heart out
sacrifice to you

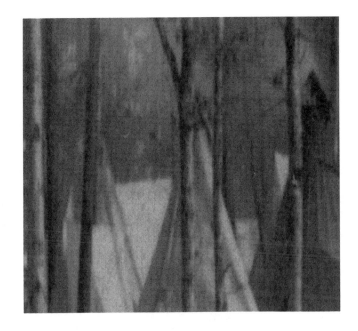

Afyonkarahisar

A handsome Jesus
you said
his arms spread out
rising with the moon
as bullets rain
olives at harvest

your boots
full of blood
there!
your face in the mud

a handsome Jesus
you said
a handsome Jesus
Hassan

The Warrior

His sward draws dances
with comrades he never kissed

concentric circles
squeeze his soul

he pulses

wingless angels
touch his lips

he smiles
νενικήθημεν

Resistance

The angels alight on his handsome face
his knurled hands

one more time

his eyes resist
the sun the ocean the mountain
they threaten
ancient myths

The lords above

He lifted his sward
in the shape of the tent

liquid light weighing
pressing forward

the dance below
numbed the sinews
the gates of tranquility
unlatched
pause

the dance below
eternal
repeated

he lifted his sward again
the lords above knew
but not of the dance below

Ripples

Red poppies in May
ooze darkness

dream ripples
distort
frozen light
pour out
swirling mandibles

Slow my God

Billions of billions
suction salutes
stings of tiny fires
rain on my body

a speck in a song I will never hear

a brick of a monstrous god
that falls in a senseless spin
when my song dies

I am

I sink as I sail magnificently

The sky below me black
cribriform

supine chest plates of Chalkis
copper
float by
hugging
Macedonian youths
in Eurotas' reeds

I sink as I sail magnificently

The mana

You said
Show me!

Fierce hawk
Your eyes sea blue

In the room
Priestesses come and go
Russia Bulgaria the Baltic

Watch the Arab boy
Shower in camels blood
And tear their flesh

Ocean blood

Tonight there is no moon

Giant Euboean kuros rises
His muddy neck shudders
Seaweeds Gorgons and Mega-Alexanders

And ocean blood surges
In the veins of sleeping boys

The making of eunuchs

Leaden mist the Euboean sea ahead of us
The moon half and feeble
Drags the terror of men
Deep into the throat of Euripos

I want the Light!
you said
I want the blue Thalassa!

But your eyes
With Euboea who moans and crackles
Shake

See the Euboean kouros on horseback
Battling witch Virgin Maries
That turn boys into eunuchs
As they dream

O lente, lente currite noctis equi!

I am condensing into a dot
I push to pass to annihilation
On the bank across
But your eyes
Solid marble

Ancient Mariner

to Giorgos Dardanos

I Alone
in a vast ocean

tracking the moon
swing slow
over the land of the pharaohs
rise
magnificent over Orchomenos
again

now swinging
dragging hordes of silent souls
simmering in swirling swamps
of scum and excrement

I must defoul my soul

in the throbbing plains of Amorgos
in the roots of the Cretan mountain
whispering winds awake
a song of ancient warriors

Spyridon

An excess of bay leaves
in my dinner tonight

too much Macedonian wine/I know
 I dribble/wisdom

an old man passed an ugly face
hell who am I he said

caught him gave him poison

then came an American I'm British he said
he threw a fistful of dung to my face
a mod of feet only feet I could see
marched over me

a gust of wind black thick and silent
hugged me
Death

then came a German who said I am oriental
you listen to ugly face old hag he said
the feet he said the feet!

It is cold tonight

I climbed Ithome
here three miles north

nude

raised my arms

eeeeeeeeeeeeeh!
eeeeeeeeeeeeeeeeeeeeeeh!
a cry a bugle

the angel of God
crucified
INVI
Ek Serron Spyridon!

eeeeeeeeeeeeeeeh!
Eeeeeeeeeeeeeeeeeeeeeeeeee!
Ευλογημένος!
blessed be Ηε! Blessed be!

the victim on the altar
was chewing on olive branches
Heraclitus
he smiled at me cunningly

the angel howled incessantly
toh! toh! toooooh!

agonizing huge battle

toooooh! tooooooooh!
a monstrous swing
Sparta Orchomenos
toooooh! tooooooooh!

a giant arm split the sky
thunder shook the mountain
now the angel sang erotically

tooooo! tooooooooh!
to Onoma Tou!

and I swooned.

The Mad Piper's Complaint
to Bill Millin

Were I a warrior
I'd pipe by your side
wade the shores of Normandy
to a soldier's death

Were I a poet
I'd write songs
of highland lads
piping savage beauty
and love

an old man I am

I hung my pipe on the wall
my fingers fumble
fading faces
of friends forgotten
on foreign lands
endlessly

a tingle down my spine
a tear

these I can

Elpenor

He looks at me in between long naps
with half closed eyes no doubt he knows
Peritas is gone so is Hercules

Elpenor drops his warrior look
his eyelids droop
he tilts his head and pleads
come back

My nightmare even to hell
to see Elpenor tied in a tin barrel

It is then when I dream of Alexander and
     Hephaestion
 naked
 running drunk with manhood in the planes
     of Troy
 mad at the mocking Gods
 Running circles around the tomb
of Achilles.

 A dog curled on the wet earth, Peritas!

 I call him
 not even a blink

Peritas! Elpenor! Hercules!
Not a wag, not a wink.

A Spartan king with a yellow parasol
walked majestically along the beach
on that cold December evening in Attica
dragging a pair of oars in the sand

Rizitika Parapezoula

Now the soldiers
tread up the slopes of Olympus
One night they'll come to your yard
to ask of Fatherland

Be on the watch

dig up earth beds in the garden
to lay their arms for the night

raise your arms
let out the horror inside you
cry out your wildest cry

Eeeeeeeeeeeeh! Eeeeeeeeeeeeh! Eeeeeeeh!

Watch that your song does not break
and the ocean wind falls
and their souls are lost in the swamp
of scum and excrement

In the deep darkness you are in

be on the watch

Elegy To A Young Whale

Farewell fellow mariner
godspeed

back into the darkness of the deep
the horror and the ecstasy

where God reigns

The River

It is when
talking of myself
I become aware
that I speak of a river of souls
of men and women and animals
living and dead

it is then
that the word
becomes unbearably heavy.

Saint George the Dragon

We too stood
At the crossroads chapel
Of Saint George killing the dragon

Dumb night our eyes
Friend
 the north
Yours to the south

And the stone

Oh stranger, tell the
Spartans Leonidas fell alone

In the tavernas men eat mushrooms in stealth

Women at home
Their pants off before the icons
Dress
Saint George the Dragon

49 FAR PITCHED TENTS-POEMS OF WAR

About the author

Michael Nikoletseas is the author of books in Medicine, Philosophy, the Classics and Mathematics. He has also written fiction and poetry. A list of his books can be found in the catalogs of libraries of Harvard, Cambridge, Oxford, Princeton Universities.

Credits

The images in this book come from the USA
Library of Congress. All of the images are
public domain. All of the images have been
edited.

53 FAR PITCHED TENTS-POEMS OF WAR

Made in the USA
Columbia, SC
17 August 2023

21757322R00030